Paddington
On the River

CARNIVAL

One morning, Paddington was woken early by the sound of voices. They seemed to be coming from somewhere outside his window, and as he climbed out of bed he helped himself to some marmalade — just to make sure he wasn't still dreaming.

When he peered out of his window he found to his surprise that all the Brown family were gathered round a large box-like object in the middle of the lawn.

It was all very mysterious and it definitely needed investigating; so without further ado, he put on his duffle-coat and hurried downstairs.

He joined the others just as Mrs. Bird was shutting the lid on a large wicker basket.

"Trust Paddington!" said Jonathan.

"It was meant to be a surprise," groaned Judy.

"Don't worry, Paddington!" laughed Mrs. Brown, when she saw the look on his face. "We're only going for a picnic on the river."

"And guess what?" said Judy. "Daddy's giving a prize to whoever catches the first fish of the day!"

Paddington had never been on a picnic before, let alone on a river, and he was very excited.

He had a quick bath and then, while Jonathan and Judy looked for some fishing nets, he made a special sandwich with the rest of his marmalade and put it under his hat in case of an emergency.

It was a very gay party of Browns who arrived at the boathouse.

"I'll put you in charge of the pole, Paddington," called Mr. Brown, as they climbed into a punt.

"Thank you very much, Mr. Brown," said Paddington. "Bears are good at poles."

"Right!" called Mr. Brown, when they were all settled. "Cast off! Anchors aweigh!"

"Do *what*, Mr. Brown?" called Paddington.

"Put the end of the pole in the water and push," shouted Jonathan.

"Oh, dear," said Mrs. Brown, as the boat began to move. "I'm sure something awful is going to happen. . . ."

Paddington did as he was told, and as soon as he felt the end of the pole touch bottom he shoved at it with all his might.

The words were hardly out of her mouth when her worst fears were realised.

Paddington discovered it was one thing pushing a pole into the bed of a river, but quite another matter getting it out again.

It was well and truly stuck in the mud.

"Help!" he cried, as he felt the punt glide away from under him.

"Mercy me!" cried Mrs. Bird.

"*Do* something, Henry!" gasped Mrs. Brown.

"*Do* something?" said Mr. Brown crossly. "What *can* I do? Paddington's got the pole!"

"Hold on, Paddington!" shouted Jonathan.

"Hold on to *what*?" gasped Paddington, as he came up for air.

Mrs. Bird lowered her sunshade.

"We'd best be using this as a paddle," she said. "I'm not sure if that bear can swim!"

At the sound of her words, Paddington gave another cry of alarm.

"I don't think I can, Mrs. Bird," he cried, and promptly sank again.

Luckily he was near the bank and some passers-by rushed to his rescue.

Soon Paddington had quite a crowd round him.

"The thing is," said a man, "'oo's going to be the first to give 'im the kiss of life?"

"Perhaps," said another man, when no one answered, "we should try artificial respiration?"

Paddington sat up.

"*Artificial* respiration!" he exclaimed hotly. "I'd rather have the real thing if you don't mind."

While he was talking, Paddington reached up to adjust his hat; and as he did so he had yet another shock.

There was nothing on his head to adjust!"

"Oh, dear," said a man, as Paddington fell over backwards in alarm. "He's lost his balance. Perhaps it's delayed shock."

"I haven't lost my balance!" said Paddington, giving the man a hard stare. "I've lost my hat. It's a very valuable one. There isn't another one like it in the world."

"Perhaps it's sunk?" suggested someone in the crowd.

"Or got swep' over the weir," said another, gloomily.

Paddington scrambled to his feet.

"My hat . . . swep' over a weir!" he exclaimed, hardly able to believe his ears.

"Don't worry, Paddington!" called Judy, as the Browns' boat drifted closer to the bank. "We'll find it."

"Jump on board," shouted Jonathan. "We'll give you a lift to the lock."

"I think," he announced over his shoulder, "I'd sooner stick to dry land, if you don't mind. It's much quicker and it's a lot safer."

Paddington considered the matter for a moment before setting off in great haste down the towpath.

"**I** knew Paddington would be upset," said Mrs. Bird, as the Browns made haste to follow him.

"He had a special bath this morning and *two* in one day is more than enough for any bear — even if one of them was an accident."

"A *hat*?" repeated the lock-keeper, when Paddington reported his loss.

"What sort of a hat?"

"It's a family heirloom," said Paddington, "and it's very special. It was handed down to me by my uncle and I've worn it ever since I left Darkest Peru."

The lock-keeper looked most impressed. "I don't think I've ever had anything from Darkest Peru over my weir before," he said.

"It wouldn't be that thing in the bucket, would it? We fished it out just now." He gave a shudder. "All dark and shapeless, it was."

"That *sounds* like it," said Mrs. Brown, as she arrived on the scene.

"I do hope so," said Mrs. Bird. "We shall never hear the last of it if it isn't."

Paddington lifted the object out of the bucket and held it up.

"It *is* my hat," he announced, much to everyone's relief.

"You can tell it's mine," he added, as he removed the remains of something white, "because it's got a marmalade sandwich inside. At least, what's left of it!"

He glanced down into the bucket again and as he did so, he nearly fell over backwards with surprise.

"**G**uess what, Mr. Brown!" he exclaimed excitedly. "I think I may have won the prize for the first catch of the day."

"Good heavens!" Mr. Brown joined Paddington at the bucket. "He's right, you know. Come and have a look, everyone."

Sure enough, as the others gathered round the bucket they could see, not one, but two fish swimming in and out of the weed at the bottom.

"You just can't compete with *that*," said Jonathan.

"*And* he got a free hat-wash into the bargain," agreed Judy.

"I expect that's how he caught the fish in the first place," remarked Mrs. Brown. "They probably swam into it by mistake."

"I expect they were hungry," said Mrs. Bird. "Fish like nibbling a piece of bread."

Paddington suddenly had second thoughts about his sandwich.

"Perhaps I won't have my elevenses after all," he announced. "I don't want to spoil my picnic. Picnics make you hungry — especially when you have them out of doors!"

This story comes from COMINGS AND GOINGS
AT NUMBER 32
and is based on the television film. It has
been specially written by Michael Bond
for younger children.

Carnival

An imprint of the Children's Division, part of
HarperCollins Publishers Ltd
77-85 Fulham Palace Road,
Hammersmith, London W6 8JB

Published by Carnival 1989

This impression 1991

ISBN 0 00 194538 6

Printed & bound in Great Britain by
BPCC Hazell Books, Paulton and Aylesbury